BRAM STOKER'S

DRACULA

A GRAPHIC NOVEL

BY MICHAEL BURGAN &
JOSÉ ALFONSO OCAMPO RUIZ

STONE ARCH BOOKS
A CAPSTONE IMPRINT

Graphic Revolve is published by Stone Arch Books
A Capstone Imprint
1710 Roe Crest Drive, North Mankato, Minnesota 56003
www.capstonepub.com

Cataloging-in-Publication Data is available at the Library of Congress website.
Hardcover ISBN: 978-1-4965-0013-7
Paperback ISBN: 978-1-4965-0032-8

Summary: On a business trip to Transylvania, Jonathan Harker stays at an eerie castle owned by a man named Count Dracula. When strange things start to happen, Harker investigates and finds the count sleeping in a coffin! Harker isn't safe, and when the count escapes to London, neither are his friends.

Common Core back matter written by Dr. Katie Monnin.

Color by Protobunker Studio.

Designer: Bob Lentz
Assistant Designer: Peggie Carley
Editor: Donald Lemke
Assistant Editor: Sean Tulien
Creative Director: Heather Kindseth
Editorial Director: Michael Dahl
Publisher: Ashley C. Andersen Zantop

Printed and bound in China. PO4399

TABLE OF CONTENTS

ABOUT VAMPIRES

Legends of vampires have haunted people for thousands of years. In fact, author Bram Stoker spent seven years researching the many tales about these creepy creatures for his book, *Dracula*.

No one knows who told the first vampire stories, but ancient Mesopotamians (meh-soh-puh-TAY-mee-ahns) were some of the first. More than 4,000 years ago, these people, from the area of modern-day Iraq, feared an evil goddess called Lamastu. The Mesopotamians believed Lamastu was responsible for many diseases including the death of young children.

Researchers have found tales of blood-sucking creatures all over the world. Most modern legends, however, come from eastern Europe. In fact, many believe the term "vampire" comes from a Russian creature called Upir (oo-PEER).

Some myths about vampires are no longer common. For example, eastern Europeans once believed that scattering seeds on the ground could keep vampires away. They thought vampires would stop to count the seeds instead of chasing after their next victim.

Some people believe author Bram Stoker named his character Dracula after a real-life person. In the mid-1400s, Prince Vlad Tepes ruled over what is today Romania. This evil leader was also known as Vlad Dracula, meaning "Son of the Dragon," and he was known for extreme cruelty toward his enemies.

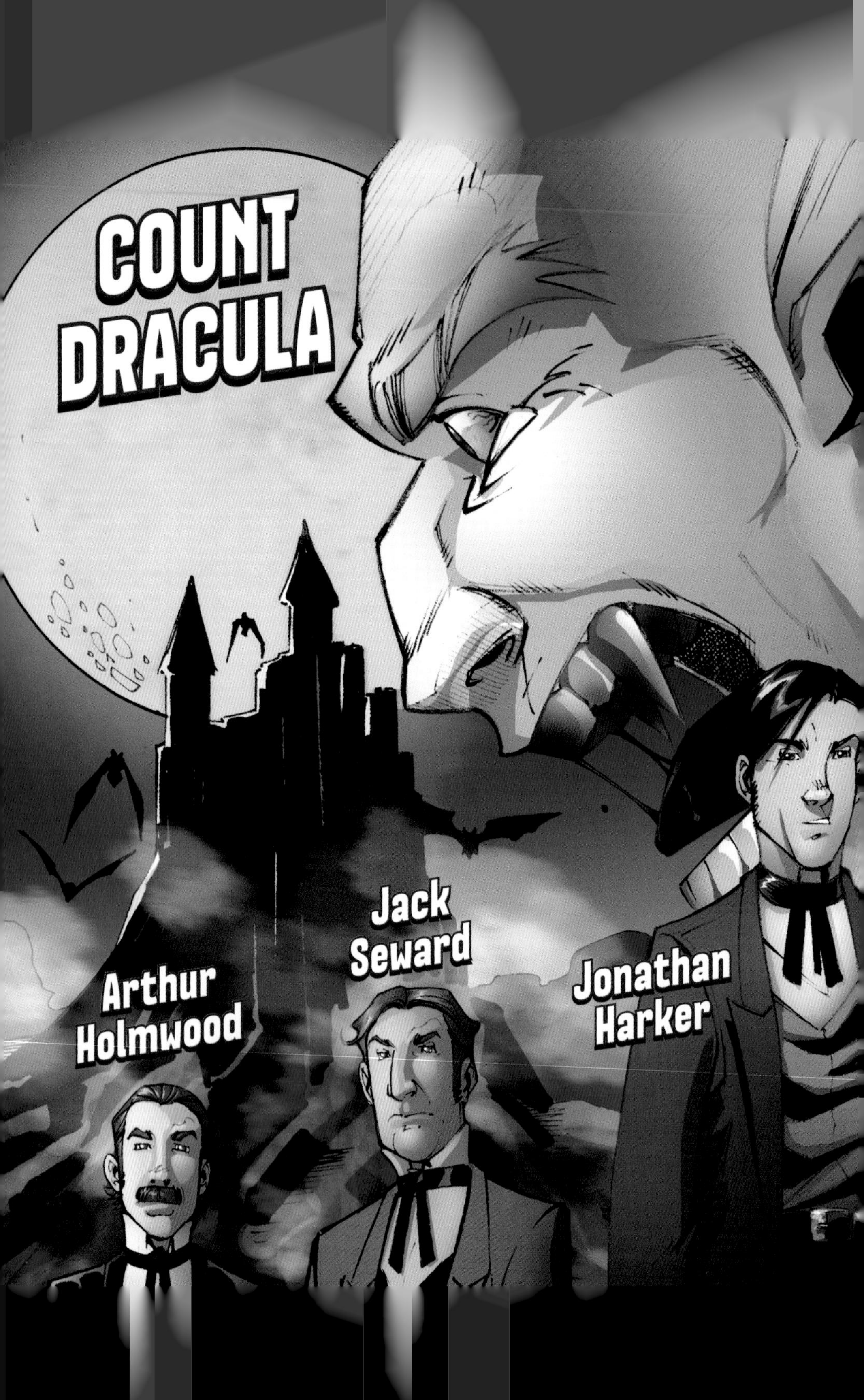
COUNT DRACULA
Jack Seward
Arthur Holmwood
Jonathan Harker

Lucy Westenra
Dr. Van Helsing
Mina Murray

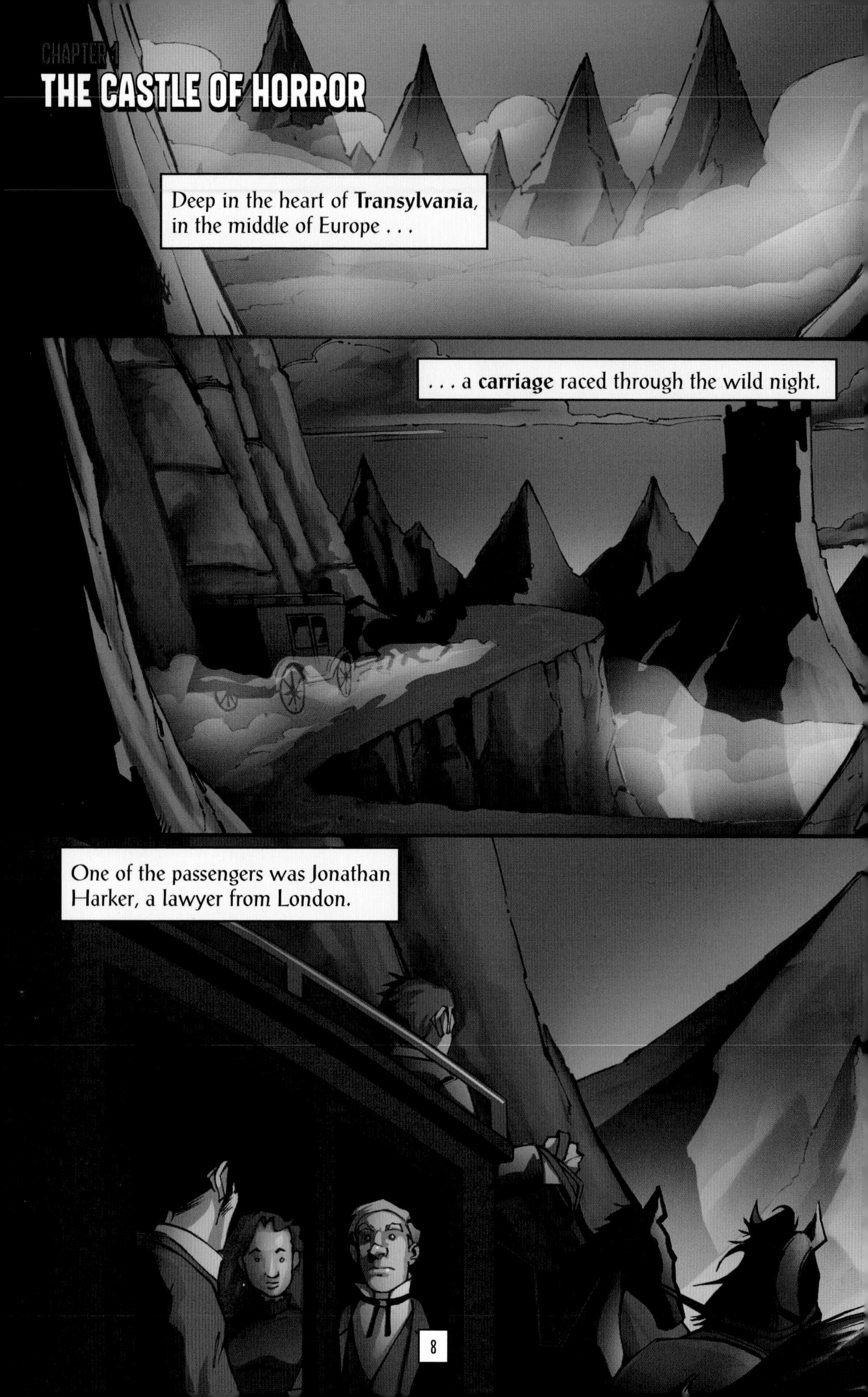
CHAPTER 1
THE CASTLE OF HORROR
Deep in the heart of Transylvania, in the middle of Europe . . .
. . . a carriage raced through the wild night.
One of the passengers was Jonathan Harker, a lawyer from London.

What brings you to our country, Mr. Harker?
My company has sent me to meet with a local man. He wishes to move to England and needs help finding a home.
Perhaps you know him? His name is Count Dracula.
Dracula?!
Lord save us!

I beg you not to go, sir!
Evil things happen at his castle.
I have no choice. He's hired my company to work for him.
Then wear this. Please. It will protect you.
The couple got off at the next stop, and the **carriage** continued toward Castle Dracula.
HOWWLLLL!!!
When Jonathan finally arrived . . .
BANG!
BANG!
BANG!

CREEEEEAAKK!
Welcome to my home, Mr. Harker.
I am Count Dracula!

You must be tired from your long journey.
I have some food and a bed waiting for you.
Thank you, Count, for everything.
He certainly is strange, but I'm sure he's harmless enough.
Early the next morning, Jonathan was getting ready before the sun came up . . .
Mr. Harker?

Count!
You **startled** me. I didn't see you in the mirror.
Are you all right? What's that on your cheek?
Blood!
You should be more careful, Mr. Harker.
Ah! No!
Did that really happen? My cross seemed to burn him.

As his visit wore on, Jonathan wanted to explore the castle.
Go anywhere you wish, Mr. Harker.
But please, do not disturb any locked rooms.
Of course.
Jonathan was too **curious** to obey Dracula.
All of them locked, except for mine.
I haven't seen a single servant with a key. A castle this big should have servants.
Am I alone in this giant castle?

Then, Jonathan discovered that the doors leading outside were locked as well.
Why is the count keeping me here?
When Harker returned to his room . . .
What is that?
It's the count!
He's climbing down that wall like a lizard on a rock!
This is madness!
I have to find a way out of here!

The next day, Jonathan snuck into Dracula's room to search for a key.
Soon . . .
No key anywhere, but where do these stairs lead?
Coffins!
The room is filled with coffins!
It's the count!
He is not human!
Jonathan decided he must return to London as quickly as possible.

That evening . . .
I must leave for London tomorrow.
I shall go with you. Get some rest and we'll leave in the morning.
Harker returned to his room, but he could not sleep. He heard voices outside his door.
What's going on out there?
JONATHAN!!
JONATHAN!!
Come to us. Become one of us!
Yes, Jonathan, we know you've learned our secret.
Noooo!
SLAM!

The count will never let me leave this place.
He plans to go to London without me.
The next morning, Jonathan returned to the room of coffins.
No, I will not let it happen.
The count now looked much younger!
I won't let him get to London.

I must destroy him!
WHACK!
ARRGH!
But the count was not destroyed so easily.
Run all you want, Jonathan!
You will never leave this place!

CHAPTER 2
DANGERS IN THE NIGHT
Back in England, Mina Murray, Jonathan's girlfriend, waited patiently for him to return. That summer, she visited her old friend, Lucy Westenra.
Oh, Mina, it's so good to see you again.
Thank you for inviting me here to Whitby.
I needed to get away from the city.
It's hard being in London with Jonathan so far away.
He almost never writes, and I worry about him.
Enough about my troubles. How are you, Lucy?

You won't believe it, but two men have asked me to marry them!
Who are they?
One is Arthur Holmwood. His father is very wealthy.
The other is a friend of Arthur's, a doctor named Jack Seward.
You must like one more than the other.
You're right! I'm going to marry Arthur.
Let me tell you all about my wedding plans.

Meanwhile, out at sea, a ship sailed for London.
Storm clouds battered the waves.
Worst weather I've seen in all my days of sailing.
If I wasn't getting paid so much to deliver this cargo, I'd head back to **Transylvania.**
The sailors didn't realize that the cargo below deck was more dangerous than any storm.

When the ship reached London a few days later . . .
Look! The ship's sails are shredded!
Where is everyone?
Suddenly, from the ship's empty deck . . .
ROOAAARRR!!
Ahh!
What is that thing?!
It looks like a wolf!
RUFF!

Later that night . . .
What was that noise?
Lucy!
What is she doing in the garden this late at night?
She must be sleepwalking.
Mina followed her friend into the garden.

By the time she got there . . .
Lucy!
RARR!
Suddenly, the evil creature vanished!
Lucy!
Are you all right?
Yes, I think so.

What was that thing?
I didn't see anything.
I thought I saw something bite you.
It's probably just a scratch, Mina. But I feel tired, so very —
Let's get you back to the house. You'll feel better tomorrow.
26

The next morning . . .
Lucy, those marks on your neck are almost gone.
Yes, it's as if last night was just a bad dream.
What's that, Mina?
A letter about Jonathan.
He was found wandering in the woods in **Transylvania.**
Now he's in the hospital. I must go see him, but I hate to leave you.
Nonsense. My friend Jack will be here any day now.
In a few days . . .
Jack, I knew you'd come.
When I heard what happened to you, I asked another doctor to come along as well.

This is Dr. Van Helsing. He'll take a look at you.
I don't know why you are so worried. I'm sure it's nothing.
We shall see, Miss Lucy. Your face is so pale.
What is this?!

!

She is in great danger, and perhaps we all are.
I must return to my office. Can someone stay with her?
The servants can watch Lucy tonight. I'll be back tomorrow morning.
That night . . .
Ahh!
Who's there?
SMASH!
WOOOOOSH!!
Lucy thought she was dreaming as the dark figure changed before her.
What is happening?
Help!

The next morning, Dr. Van Helsing and Jack reached Lucy's house at almost the same time.
All the doors are locked, Doctor!
We might already be too late. We must go through a window.
Inside, the men found Lucy's servants asleep.
What happened?
They're under some kind of spell.
Quickly, upstairs!
Lucy!

Is she alive?
Barely.
And look here!
Dr. Van Helsing gently parted Lucy's lips.
Evil is at work!

CHAPTER 3
A MYSTERIOUS DEATH
The next day, Dr. Van Helsing returned to check on Lucy. Jack had watched her through the night.
You'll never believe it. Lucy's neck is fine!
What?!
Does this mean she's better?
I'm afraid not, Jack.
It means we can do nothing for her now.
Meanwhile in London . . .
Jonathan, I'm so glad you've come home. I can't wait to tell Lucy!
Yes, and soon we'll –
I don't believe it!
What is it, dear?

I think I see Count Dracula!
No, it can't be him!
What's wrong?
I want you to read my **journal**.
You should know everything I saw at the count's castle.
When they got home, Mina found a note waiting for them.
It's from a Dr. Van Helsing.
He was taking care of Lucy.
She's sick?
Oh, Jonathan! She is dead!

Van Helsing had read Lucy's diary and learned about the strange beast in the garden.
The doctor is coming here tomorrow.
He thinks I might be able to help him understand what happened to Lucy.
And Jonathan? I think I should read your journal tonight.
The next day, Van Helsing arrived.
I know you're here about Lucy, but I must ask you something about Jonathan, too.
This is his journal. Please read it, Doctor.
He has not been well!

That afternoon . . .
Did you read the journal? Is Jonathan crazy, Doctor?
He is not crazy, Mina.
Who's not crazy?
You, Jonathan.
I have read your journal, and you were lucky to escape that castle.
Now, however, I believe that Count Dracula is here in England.
Dracula must be stopped! He is a dangerous man.
I will hunt him down, but I need your help.
Van Helsing took all of the papers Mina had given him and headed back to Lucy's home in the country.

At the train station, a newspaper story caught Dr. Van Helsing's eye.
No!
This can't be! I must tell Jack Seward!
When he reached Lucy's house . . .
Jack! Read this!
What's wrong, Doctor?
Just read it!
"We have received reports that several local people were found early in the morning with strange marks on their necks!"

Strange marks on their necks.
Just like the ones we saw on Lucy.
Do you think the same creature that attacked Lucy bit these others?
It's much worse than that, Jack.
Lucy made these marks herself.
Lucy has become a vampire!

Dr. Van Helsing, that is impossible!
There are creatures who are not alive, and yet not dead.
They are known as the **undead**, such as vampires.
There is an **undead** creature here in England, and Lucy was his first victim.
Now she is a vampire and needs blood. It is like food and water to her.
What can we do?

Van Helsing led Jack to the cemetery where Lucy Westenra was buried.
WESTENRA

This is madness!
What do you expect to find in here?
Nothing!
Because at night, a vampire must go out and search for blood.
LUCY
The coffin was empty, just as the doctor had predicted.
The two men went back out into the cemetery . . . and waited.
Perhaps someone stole her body.
Perhaps, but I doubt it. Let's stay for a while and see what happens.
Several hours passed. Then suddenly, Van Helsing saw something in the distance.
Over there!

Hurry!
As the men raced near, the shadowy creature escaped.
That figure must have been Lucy!
She stole this child and would have hurt him if we had not been here.
Should we tell Arthur about this?
Yes.
Then we'll tell him we must destroy Lucy once and for all, as only a vampire can be destroyed.

The next day, Lucy's love, Arthur, finally arrived. Jack and Dr. Van Helsing told him what they had seen.
Jack, this is crazy!
Do you really believe in vampires?
I didn't before last night.
I know this is hard, Arthur.
Perhaps you should come see for yourself.
After the sun had set . . .
It was just about this time last night –
Look! Over there!
WESTENRA

Lucy?
No! It can't be!
We must let Lucy go back to her **tomb**. Then we wait until morning.
She will lose her strength when the sun is up.
ESTENRA

In the early hours of morning . . .
What are those things in the bag for?
It's the only way to kill a vampire.
My poor Lucy!
It is not the Lucy you once knew.
You understand what you must do?
Y-y-yes.

WHACK!
Now, we must seal the tomb with lead, and we are done . . . for now.

Several days later, Mina and Jonathan received a letter.
It's from Dr. Van Helsing. He wants us to meet him in London.
I have business I must finish. You go, and I'll meet you there.
Oh, poor Lucy! What a horrible story!
Everything will be all right, dear Mina.
I hope so, Jonathan.
I truly hope so.

The next day, Mina arrived at Lucy's home and met with Jack Steward.
I'm not surprised this is happening, Jack.
What do you mean?
Jonathan saw terrible things in **Transylvania.**
Now these terrible things are happening here.
Jack, you must read his **journal.**

As Jack finished reading, the others arrived with Jonathan.
Mina showed me your journal, Jonathan. What an awful experience!
I hear you've had your own horrible time with Lucy.
Yes, one friend gone, and another almost dead, all because of Count Dracula.
He must be stopped!
What have you learned about him, Doctor?
He can command wolves, rats, and bats. If he wishes, he can also take the shape of these animals.
He has at least one home here in London.

I know where his new home is. It's not far from here, Doctor.
We must find the 50 boxes he shipped from Transylvania.
He can only rest in soil from his native land. Come along, gentlemen!
They soon arrived at Dracula's nearby house.
My friends, we face a terrible danger.
Before we enter this house, I have some items that will protect us.
A bottle of holy water.
A crucifix, like the one that saved Jonathan.
And a few sacred wafers. Keep them all close.

Inside Dracula's house . . .
Put some of the **sacred wafers** on each box of soil you find.
Then Dracula won't be able to sleep in them again.
Do you hear that?
Look! Down there!
SQUEAK!
SQUEAK!
SQUEAK!
QUEAK!
SQUEAK!
Rats!
Don't let them frighten you.
It's just one of the count's evil tricks.

Soon the rats disappeared, and the men searched the house carefully.
How many boxes did you find?
Fewer than fifty. He must have sent the rest to other houses.
We must contact the shipping company and track them down!

Mina tried to rest next door. When she closed her eyes, she saw only vampires.
Then she opened her eyes.
No! Stay away!
Silence! You will do as I say.
I need to drink.
Ahh!

Now it is YOUR turn. You will drink my blood.
Drink!
And now, wherever you go, you will be under my control. My mind and yours are linked.
Mina!
No!

You fools!
But then . . .
Stop, you beast!
You are too late to save her.

He's gone!
Are you all right, Mina?
I feel so strange.
We must find those other boxes tomorrow.
Then we must kill Dracula, or else —
Or else, I will become a vampire too!

That night . . .
This is the last box, men. We've placed wafers on all the others.
It's the only box that Dracula can use now.
Then he must come back here tonight.
Yes, and we'll be waiting.
As they waited . . .
Did you hear that?
Soon the men saw the front door open.

The men jumped from their hiding places.
You fools!
I have other places where I can go.
You can't stop me!
SMASH!
He's gone!

Back at Jack's house, the men explained what happened to Mina.
But we must find him. We must kill him!
We? Mina, you're so weak now. What could you do?
Dracula said that he can control me. Our minds are linked.
If Dr. Van Helsing can hypnotize me, I may be able to learn from Dracula's thoughts.
Is this possible, Doctor?

Perhaps.
Mina, I want you to relax. Feel your eyes grow heavy.
What do you see?
Nothing.
Everything is dark.
Wait! I can hear somebody talking. He's saying . . .
All the cargo is on board. Prepare to sail!
That's all. The voice is gone!
The count must have had one more box of earth.
He's trying to get back to **Transylvania**. We must follow him!

CHAPTER 7

THE END OF DRACULA

The group quickly made plans for their trip. They sailed to France, and then boarded a train.

The count's power is strong. I can feel we are getting closer to him.
You must all promise me something, even you, Jonathan.
If I start to change into what Lucy became, you must kill me!
My darling, Mina, I shall love you to the very end.

We must make certain the count will not harm you further.
This sacred wafer shall protect your mind!
Doctor! I can't even feel it!
TSSSSSSSSS

When they neared **Transylvania**, the vampire hunters learned that men had been hired to take Dracula's coffin into the mountains.
We should split up.
You three, follow the boat. Mina and I will try to reach the count's castle before he gets there.
Hours later, Dr. Van Helsing and Mina could no longer see the road ahead of them. They were forced to pull over and camp for the night.
After they had lit their campfire . . .
Doctor! Who are they?
Do not fear, Mina. The holy wafers will keep these creatures from reaching us.

Mina!
Come, dear sister.
Join us!
Pray for sunlight, Mina!
These monsters will flee at daybreak.
The holy wafers wouldn't keep the creatures away much longer.
Jonathan, save us!

Jonathan and the others followed Dracula's wagon as it neared the castle.
Halt!
Unload the coffin, so we can search it.
Suddenly, Dracula rose from the fallen coffin.
Arrgghh!

This is for Lucy. And for Mina!
Noooo!
Just then . . .
Your forehead! The burn from the wafer is gone.
Jonathan did it! Dracula has been destroyed!
The power of the evil Count Dracula was gone . . . forever!

ABOUT THE RETELLING AUTHOR AND ILLUSTRATOR

Michael Burgan has written many fiction and nonfiction books for children. A history graduate from the University of Connecticut, Burgan worked at *Weekly Reader* for six years before beginning his freelance writing career. He has received an award from the Educational Press Association of America and has won several playwriting contests. He lives in Chicago with his wife, Samantha.

José Alfonso Ocampo Ruiz was born in 1975 in Macuspana, Tabasco in Mexico, where the temperature is just as hot as the sauce is. He became a comic book illustrator when he was 17 years old, and has worked on many graphic novels since then. Alfonso has illustrated several graphic novels, including retellings of *Dracula* and *Pinocchio*.

GLOSSARY

carriage (KAIR-ij)—a small vehicle with wheels, often pulled by horses

crucifix (KRU-sih-fiks)—a cross, which Christians believe represents Jesus Christ

curious (KYUR-ee-uhss)—a strong desire to investigate

journal (JUR-nuhl)—a book or notebook where someone records the daily events of his or her life, such as a diary

sacred wafer (SAY-krid WAY-fur)—a round, thin piece of bread often given during a Christian church service

startled (STAR-tuhld)—frightened by being surprised

tomb (TOOM)—a place for holding a dead body

Transylvania (tran-sil-VAIN-yuh)—a real-life mountainous region in eastern Europe

undead (un-DED)—another name for a vampire or zombie

vampire (VAM-pire)—a dead person believed to come out of the grave at night and suck the blood of the living

COMMON CORE ALIGNED
READING QUESTIONS

1. **Chapter 1 is titled "The Castle of Horror." Why might the author have chosen this title? What happens in the story to make this chapter title appropriate?** *("Refer to details and examples in a text when explaining what the text says.")*

2. **Why does Mr. Harker willingly go to Count Dracula's castle? What happens to him while he is there?** *("Describe in depth a character, setting, or event in a story.")*

3. **"Horror" and "fright" are similar themes in this story. What happens in the plot to make these two themes so important?** *("Determine a theme of a story.")*

4. **Describe Count Dracula. How does he interact with other characters in the story? What do the other characters think about Count Dracula?** *("Describe in depth a character . . . drawing on specific details in the text.")*

5. **Who is Mina Murray and what is she doing while her boyfriend Jonathan Harker is stuck in Dracula's castle? Is she worried about Jonathan? How do you know?** *("Refer to details and examples in a text when explaining what the text says explicitly and when drawing inferences from the text.")*

COMMON CORE ALIGNED
WRITING QUESTIONS

1. **If you were Count Dracula and had invited Mr. Harker to stay at your castle, what would your invitation say? Write an invitation from Count Dracula to Mr. Harker. Why does he need Mr. Harker's help? What else does he tell Mr. Harker about the castle?** *("Draw evidence from literary . . . texts to support analysis.")*

2. **Do you think Count Dracula is a good host? A poor host? Would you want to stay at his castle? Why or why not?** *("Write opinion pieces on topics or texts, supporting a point of view with reasons and information.")*

3. **What is the main idea (or theme) of this graphic novel? How do you know? In two or three paragraphs, explore your answer using examples from the story.** *("Write informative/explanatory texts to examine a topic and convey ideas.")*

4. **If you were playing Count Dracula in a school play, what character traits would you want to highlight while on stage? Write a one-page journal entry explaining how you would like to portray Count Dracula.** *("Write narratives to develop real or imagined experiences or events.")*

5. **Describe Count Dracula's castle. What does it look like? If you were to stay a night in the castle, what would you see?** *("Draw evidence from literary . . . texts to support analysis.")*

READ THEM ALL!

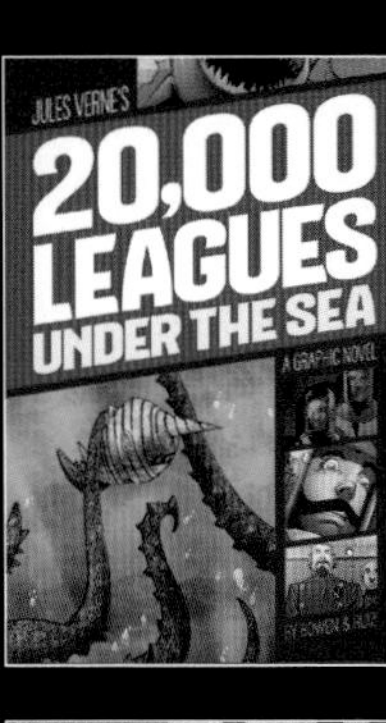

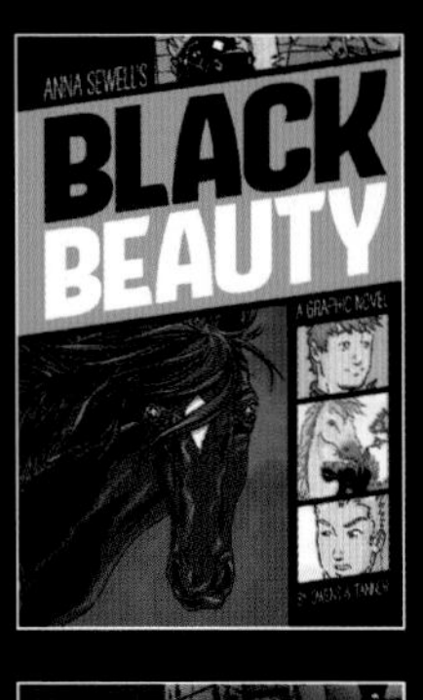

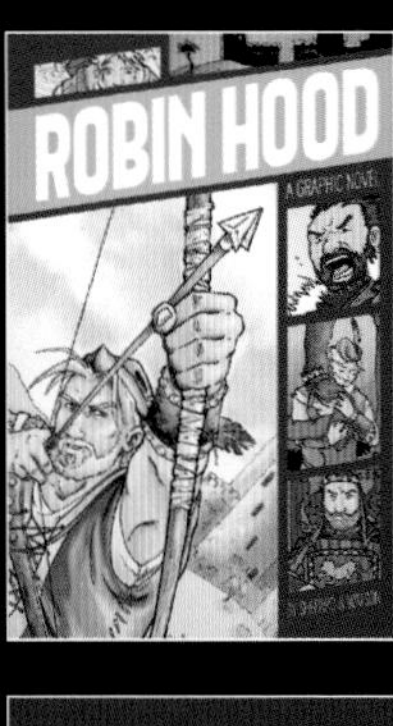

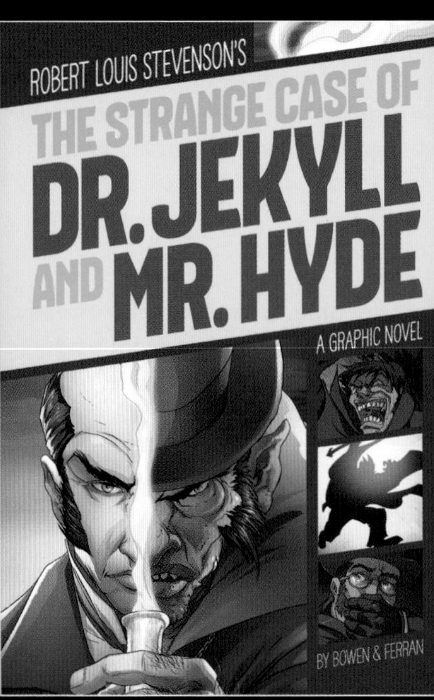

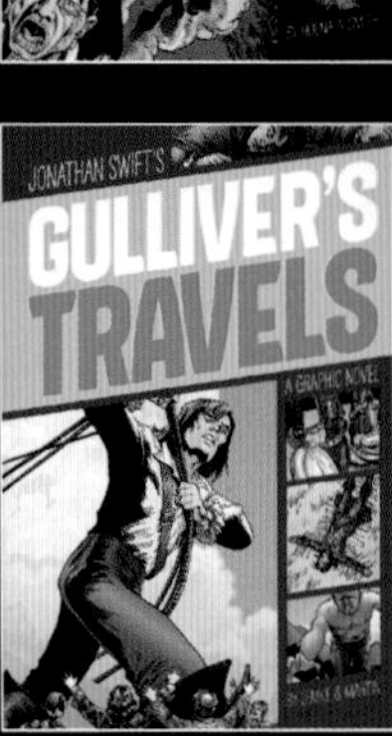

ARTHUR CONAN DOYLE'S
THE HOUND OF THE BASKERVILLES
A GRAPHIC NOVEL

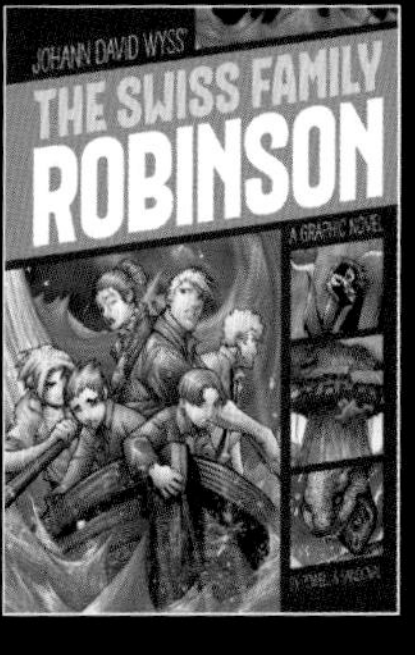
JOHANN DAVID WYSS'
THE SWISS FAMILY ROBINSON
A GRAPHIC NOVEL

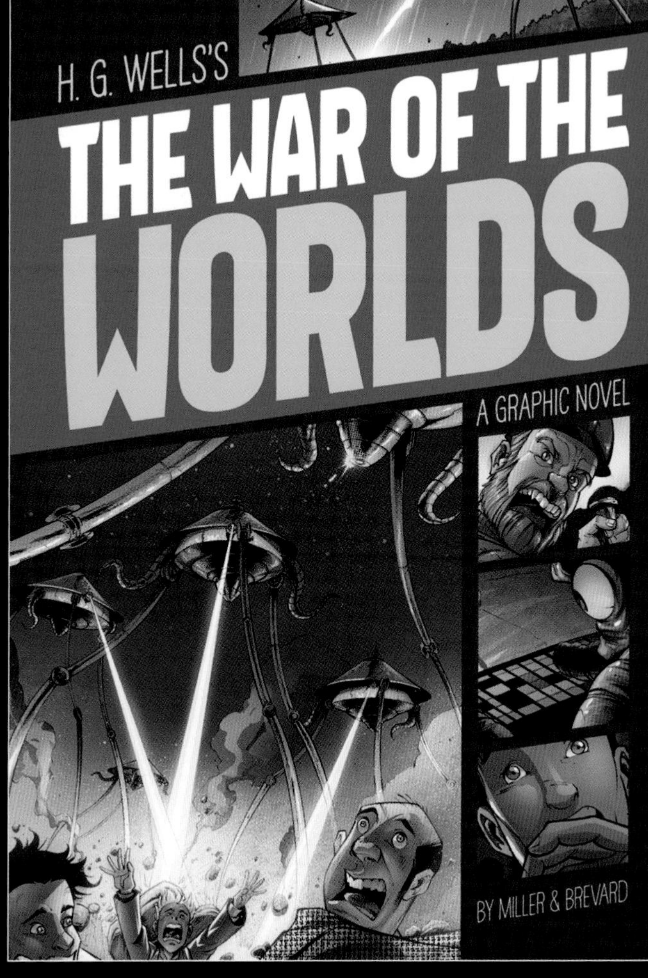
H. G. WELLS'S
THE WAR OF THE WORLDS
A GRAPHIC NOVEL
BY MILLER & BREVARD

PERSEUS AND MEDUSA
A GRAPHIC NOVEL

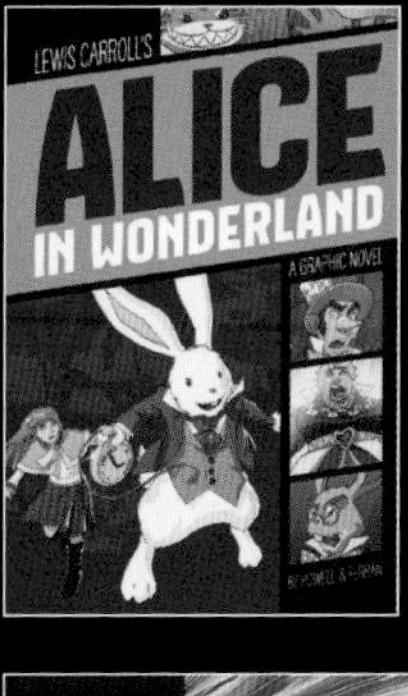
LEWIS CARROLL'S
ALICE IN WONDERLAND
A GRAPHIC NOVEL

H.G. WELLS'S
THE TIME MACHINE
A GRAPHIC NOVEL
BY DAVIS & RUIZ

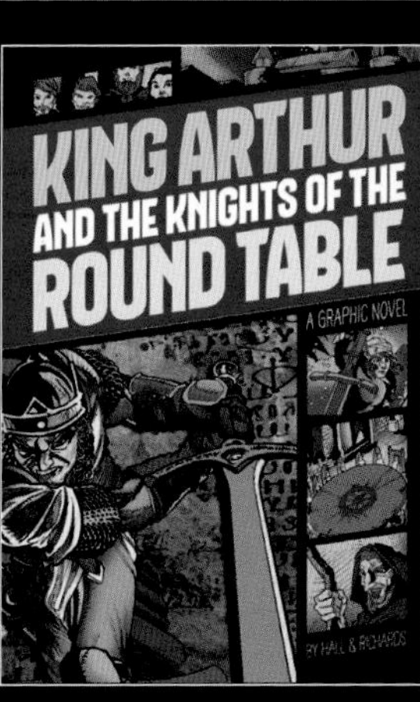
KING ARTHUR AND THE KNIGHTS OF THE ROUND TABLE
A GRAPHIC NOVEL
BY HALL & RICHARDS

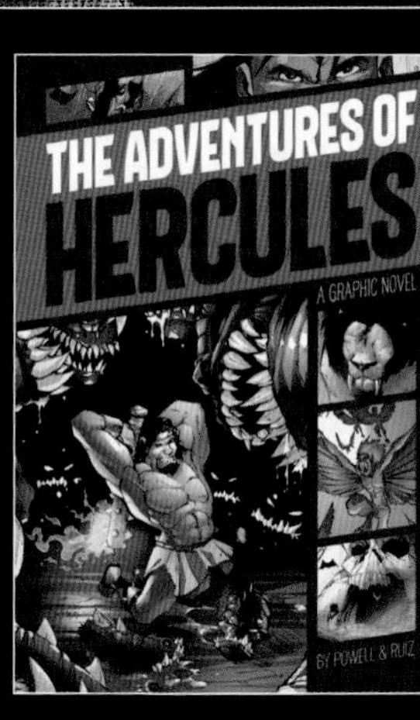
THE ADVENTURES OF HERCULES
A GRAPHIC NOVEL
BY POWELL & RUIZ